ELAINE'S ESCAPE

DISCOVERED DESIRE

HELANA PARKINS

plicit Press
Erotica Fiction

CHAPTER 1

ELAINE ROLLED over and hit the snooze button on her alarm clock. God, she hated that thing. She hated it even more today. Last night's drinking binge hadn't been such a great choice, in hindsight. Ever since she had been left by her fiancé, Tim, she hadn't really cared very much about her decisions or their results. She let out a low groan as she rolled over in her bed, her head pounding like a drum circle from Africa. She hadn't remembered tequila hurting this badly last time. But then again, last time, she hadn't drank more than half of a bottle.... AFTER she got home from the bar. At least she had made it home safely and alone. No weird situations to get out of or men to send home in a cab.

Normally, Elaine wasn't like this. She was settled, balanced and happy, with a great 9 – 5 job and an amazing fiancé whom she was going to spend the rest of her life with. He was amazing and had a fabulous job with one of the top law firms in the city. He had landed it right after passing the bar due to his father's already established connections within the city's legal community. He had swept Elaine off of her feet the moment she had met him. From a middle-class family in the suburbs, she had been quite taken with his suaveness, his smooth-talking, and his charm from the moment she had met him. Not to mention his devilishly handsome good looks. She was the envy of all the sorority girls, and they had been through numerous near-breakups, mostly attempts by other girls or boys who were jealous enough to break up their relationship.

Elaine was a good-looking girl with light brown hair that fell to her waist and was straight as a stick. Her round, blue eyes made her look far more innocent than she ever pretended to be, but it had always seemed to work in her favor, so she never complained too much. She was kind-hearted by nature, just not quite as innocent as she looked. Or so she thought anyway. Having grown up with 4 older brothers, she liked to think of herself more as one of the boys than one of the girls and that she could handle any situation as brashly and just as well as any man.

In reality, this couldn't be farther from the truth. She had grown up with 4 brothers, and she had tagged along with them whenever she could as the youngest sister. But what she didn't realize was how much they had actually protected her from and sheltered her from. That they never took her to the crass keg parties with just the boys they held late at night on the heavily forested island that graced the golf course their home backed onto. She never heard the ways in which they discussed the girls that they slept with or how they kept them from finding out about each other. There were many things her brothers sheltered her from, which was probably why she had been so shocked when Tim left her, and she realized the truth about what had been going on.

Tim had proposed to her during their last semester of college. They had a huge, elaborate wedding planned at the biggest cathedral in the city, followed by an amazing reception at the 5-star hotel down the street. The guest list was over 250 people. They had invited all of both sides of their families, from Great-Aunt May down to her newest nephew and all of their friends in between. His dress had cost her $7,000- almost as much as her car!! She was beyond excited to begin her new life with her fiancé until she went to meet him at lunch one day.

She went to their usual café spot about 10 minutes early and got them a table, waiting patiently and happily for him to arrive from work so he could spend his lunch break with her. Elaine had been so engrossed in her phone that she didn't even notice him walk up to the table. She was even more surprised when she looked up and saw him accompanied by a tall, serious-looking woman with long black hair and thin, pursed lips. She had pale skin, a very obvious boob job, and a look on her face that meant nothing but business.

Elaine didn't even know what to say or how to react when they both sat down at the table, and Tim began to speak. When he introduced her to the woman, she didn't even hear the name; she was so taken aback by what was going on.

Somehow through her shock, she had heard him say "affair," heard him calling off the wedding, and mumbling something else about it not being for him. She sat there at her table, dumbfounded and in tears long after he had told her and had left with his mistress. Elaine felt as though she had been punched in the gut. How could he have? And for how long? She had been so stupid and naïve and had thought that everything was perfect. What had she done? How could she not have seen this happening? Were there clues that she missed? Or signs? Maybe she was a bad lover? It was too much for her to bear by herself.

She called up her best friend Kristy and told her what had happened. Still sitting at the café table with her makeup smeared, she tried to compose herself as best she could.

"Oh, Kristy! What am I going to do? I don't even know where to start!" Elaine cried into the phone.

"Order yourself some ice cream, and I'll be right there," Kristy had said to her, hanging up the phone.

Moments later, Kristy had arrived at the café. Giving Elaine a big hug, she sat down at the table in the chair next to her.

"Well, look at the bright side... at least you saved yourself a big nasty divorce," Kristy said, trying to comfort her.

"What am I going to do, Kristy? The wedding is supposed to be in 2 weeks and then the honeymoon tickets. My family is coming out and his and, oh God! This is such a disaster!" Elaine said as she began to cry again.

"There, there...." said Kristy, patting Elaine on the back. "It's going to be okay. We're going to take care of this one step at a time. The first thing you need to do is call your mom and let her know so that she can handle your side of the family. And she's so awesome she'll probably handle canceling most of the wedding stuff for you as well. You know that, right? You're not going to have to do this alone."

"What about your honeymoon trip. Are you still going to go on it? You have the tickets... I think you should," Kristy insisted.

"Oh God, I'm far too depressed to be taking a vacation by myself right now, Kristy." Elaine began to protest.

"Oh, I wasn't thinking that you would go by yourself. Change his tickets to my name, and I'll go with you! We'll have an excellent time and forget all about Tim. Oh, come on, let's!! It'll be so much fun!!

"You know.... That's actually not a bad idea. It'll be a good way to take my mind off of everyone who isn't coming out here. Plus, it is Jamaica...." Elaine trailed off.

"That's the spirit!!" Kristy gave her another big hug. "Let's pay the bill and get out of here."

Kristy threw down a fifty on the table and looked at her friend. "That should cover it, right? I don't feel like waiting for change."

"Oh that should be more than enough," Elaine replied as she picked up her purse and followed Kristy out of the restaurant. Relieved to be moving on, even if she wasn't sure in what direction yet.

Over the following two weeks, her best friend Kristy and her mother were more than amazing in helping her to get the word out and cancel all of the plans for the wedding. Everyone was very understanding and sweet, and she was given plenty of space and time to recover. Before she knew it, two weeks had passed, and it was time for her and Kristy to go on the cruise. She couldn't help but feel sad as she was packing up for the trip. All she could think about was how it was supposed to have been her happy honeymoon with Tim. She couldn't go down this road of self-pity again. What was Tim doing? NOT sitting around and moping. That was for sure. Hell, he might even be on another fancy trip with his new if she was a new girlfriend.

Hell, what was she doing? Why was she still feeling sad about this? She began to feel a new emotion besides sadness and gut-wrenching loneliness for the first time since Tim had left her at that café table in the middle of the city. She began to feel angry. Angry that he had lied to her, that he had led her on, and so horribly in front of both of their families and all of their friends, their co-workers. That woman must have been a very impressive lady for him to do what he had done. Even his family was so furious with him that his father had had him removed from the living trust. Or so she had heard. She wasn't going to sit around and feel sorry for herself anymore. Tim had been lucky that she was with him, and she would find someone else to be with all in good time. She was going to make the most of her trip and maybe even make some new friends. No more sad Elaine, no more sad Elaine at all. She decided to call Kristy and see how her packing was going since she still couldn't seem to stay focused on anything but thinking about her emotional state of mind.

'Hello?" Kristy answered the phone.

"Kristy! Are you done packing yet?" Elaine asked.

"Oh my God, no. And I still feel like I am bringing too much. Why can't I just pack a swimsuit and my toothbrush and call it good?" Kristy whined on the other end of the phone.

"Are we really supposed to be at the airport in 3 hours?"

"Yes, we are!" Elaine answered her. "And I haven't even started packing yet! I think I'm going to do a bit of shopping while we're there and just buy a bunch of new comfy clothes. Maybe even some new sexy clothes too."

"You know," Kristy said, "that's not such a bad idea. I think I'm just going to make sure I've got the bare basics and do a bunch of shopping with you."

"Yay!" Elaine said. "I'll see you at the airport in three hours then?"

"Two hours and forty-five minutes!! I just am so excited!!!" Kristy almost screamed back into the phone.

The flight had gone smoothly enough, with the typical babies crying in the back of the plane and the people dragging on their too-large carry-ons, trying to stuff them overhead or underneath the seat in front of them. None of it had bothered her, though. She was lost in thought, dreaming about her trip and her time on the boat.

Laying her head back into the upright airplane seat, she had lost herself in a daydream involving a sexy cabana boy and some strawberry daiquiris and a lot of suntan oil. Before she knew it, the plane had landed, and they were in a cab on their way to the shipyards. She had been out of the country before, but she had never been on a cruise. Not quite sure what to expect, she lost her breath as the cab rounded the corner of a large wall, and she looked up and saw the massive shape of the cruise boat in front of her.

"Kristy! It's so big!" she exclaimed, grabbing ahold of her arm, peering out of the cab window and the huge ship docked up. They watched as workers scurried back and forth at the bottom of the boat, loading on luggage, food, and other large boxes and crates. There was a ramp that the passengers were filing up slowly as they loaded into the cruise ship, many of them holding hands with their partner or children and carrying another small carry-on bag or purse in the other. The cab pulled up to the dock and let them out, pulling out their bags for them and setting them by Porter's station on the sidewalk. They hopped excitedly out of the cab and breathed in the salty sea air around them, feeling more excited than ever for their vacation.

They paid the cab driver, and he left.

"Welcome, ladies!" said the porter, dressed in his blue boat pants and button-up, short sleeve shirt. The name on his nametag said "Evrim," and his country was Turkey. He wasn't anything spectacular looking to her, but very friendly and obviously very determined to give them the best welcome possible.

Elaine smiled at him, "Thank you."

"Welcome to the Big Dream!! Where all of your dreams will come true!!" Evrim said in an exuberant tone of voice.

Elaine and Kristy smiled at each other and giggled. He was pretty intense with his act. Still, they were excited. This was going to be a heap of fun.

"If I could have your papers, please ladies?" Evrim requested as he put his hands out.

The girls rummaged in their purses, pulling out the papers that they needed, and handing them over to Evrim. He flipped through them quickly and looked at them.

"I.D. as well, please," he said, smiling at them. They dug once more and handed them over.

"Just as beautiful in your pictures as you are in real life," Evrim said.

The two girls burst out in laughter. That was too much; they both hated their driver's license pictures.

Evrim grinned at the ladies, knowing full well what he had done, and he handed them back each of their papers and I.D. "What? You don't like your picture?" he said, still smiling at the girls. "I will take care of your bags. Please just take what you need with you until dinner time. The porters will have all of the bags in the room by 4 pm, just in time to get dressed for dinner. Your suite will be room 615; it is one of our best suites on the ship. There will be papers in your cabin that should explain most of your questions, and you can simply ring the bellhop if you need anything at all. Thank you, ladies, and enjoy your time with us."

Evrim finished his talk and bowed, extending his arm down the walkway. The ladies smiled and giggled again. "Thank you, Evrim," they said to him as they walked past and up the walkway taking in the massiveness of the ship as they walked up the plank.

Upon entering the ship, they were amazed. It was more like a little city than a boat. There were people scurrying about everywhere as the giant ship was making its final preparations for departure. They were in the main lobby of the ship, which opened up and showed 3 levels above them and two below them. There was a large map on the wall that people were gathering around before then scattering off to find their destination. Kristy and Elaine waited for their turn to get close to the map so that they could locate which direction their suite was in.

Once they located it on the map, they headed off towards the port end of the big ship to find their suite. They were nearer to the top, which they had been hearing was the place to be. Elaine didn't know anything really about the suite that had been booked. Just that it was the honeymoon suite, so it had sounded pretty perfect at the time. They had looked into getting a different suite, but it was too late for them to change rooms by the time they arrived there.

Upon walking into the room, both of the girls gasped. It was not the traditional tiny cruise ship rooms that one heard about in horror from all of their friends; this was big and roomy and expansive. There was a Jacuzzi tub in the bathroom, a large King-sized bed in the middle, a lit-up vanity area, an eating nook, a mini living room, and a walkout balcony area with a chaise lounge and a couple of chairs on it for company.

"You certainly know how to do a trip, girl!" Kristy exclaimed as they entered their new home for the next week. Elaine looked around and smiled; she ran and hopped onto the big bed like a little girl.

"Look at this view!" Kristy remarked as she slid open the balcony door and looked out of their window. I bet we're going to be seeing some amazing sunrises and sunsets this week."

"Sunrises?" Elaine looked at her doubtfully.

"Yea, you know, because we'll still be up," Kristy said laughing.

Elaine laughed, "You are too much sometimes, girl, but I love you. I don't think I'll be doing too many sunrises this week, but you can count me in on all of the sunsets!!"

"I'm so excited for our ports. Where is our first destination?" Kristy asked.

"Our first destination is Cozumel, then Honduras, followed by Jamaica, and then we hit the Grand Cayman Islands on our way back," said Elaine happily, as she sprawled out on the big bed, enjoying the feel of the cool, crisp linens against her skin.

"So amazing!" said Kristy wandering back into the room off of the balcony, she began to rummage through the kitchen area.

"I wonder where the papers that tell about the boat are. Oh, here they are!" Kristy said as she located them in front of the ice bucket and coffee maker. "Let's see what all we have going on," Kristy cooed excitedly as she pulled out the map and opened it up.

"Sheesh, this boat is HUGE!! There are 7 different places to eat, 4 bars inside, 4 swim-up bars, two nightclubs, a piano/karaoke bar... look they even have a sushi restaurant!!! Every night of the week they have a different buffet, a midnight chocolate buffet, a banana split, and an ice cream Sunday buffet. There are also 3 casinos and 2 different shopping areas!!! What do you want to go explore first?" she asked.

"Let's go grab a drink and check out the bars before we get take off. I feel a little weird going to the swimming pool while everyone is still boarding and tending to business. What do you think?" Elaine suggested.

'Sounds like a great idea to me," Kristy said.

The pair grabbed their room's fobs and headed out of their suite to go explore the giant ship. They wandered around until they found a nice quiet bar near the front of the ship. They sat down at the bar and ordered a couple of drinks from the cute bartender. Before they could get too deep into their conversation they were approached by two very handsome, if not somewhat cocky, men.

"Do you mind if we join you ladies for a drink?" the blond man on the right said, as he smiled at Kristy and then at Elaine. Elaine began to look them over carefully, taking her time in trying to size them up. She wasn't impressed by their cockiness and was about to say something when Kristy interrupted her.

"Of course, we don't!" she said loudly, and much to Elaine's dismay. She forced out a smile and took a big gulp out of her drink.

"Here, let me move my purse. Y'all can sit in these two chairs right here. I'm Kristy and this is my bestie, Elaine. We're taking a girls' trip! How about you guys?" Kristy kept talking to the men, much to Elaine's horror. She took another gulp of her drink and let the warmth from the alcohol flow through her body. She decided to relax and let her reservations go. After all, she was on vacation and what harm would a little bit of company do them?

"My name is Evan," said the blond man as he sat down next to Kristy, shaking her hand and then Elaine's. "It's a pleasure to meet you ladies. And thank you for letting us join you. This here is my brother, Hank. He's not quite as much of a talker as I am. We're here for a boy's week of relaxing as well. And we're very much looking forward to it.

Have you ladies picked your adventures at the ports of call yet?" Evan continued excitedly.

Elaine looked past him as he rambled on, and caught the eye of his brother Hank who smiled at her quietly; she felt as though he agreed with her feelings and perhaps had some of his own. He didn't seem quite as irritating as his brother, now that they were both sitting down. And he was cuter than she had first allowed herself to see. His light brown hair hung shaggily over his dark brown eyes, he had a subdued yet sweet smile. There was something that made her want to know him, maybe just a little more.

Elaine couldn't really think of anything to say, and obviously, Hank couldn't either. Kristy and Evan continued to yap while the two of them sat and nursed their drinks slowly. Elaine gave Hank a half-smile; it had been so long since she had dated anyone. She had totally lost her game at this point.

"Shots?" Elaine suggested as she looked at Hank.

"That sounds like a great idea!" Hank replied, springing to life a bit.

"Why don't you come sit over here closer to me? That way it's easier to talk to you."

Elaine got up and walked over to the barstool next to Hank and hopped up on it, realizing how much larger his frame was than her own petite one.

"What shots shall we order?" Hank asked her.

Elaine smiled a bit deviously... "How do you feel about a nice shot of tequila?" "Oooooh, someone's a tough Girl," Hank said to her teasingly.

"Bartender, two shots of your best reposado tequila, chilled and with a clamato back," Elaine ordered across the bar.

Hank looked at her, a bit shocked, a smile spreading

across his face. "She knows what she wants and how to get it too," he said.

Elaine looked at him and smiled back. "That is very true," said Elaine. "For the most part."

"Oh I bet a girl like you always gets her way," Hank said to her.

She felt some pangs of sadness come up and she stuffed them back down again, trying not to focus on how she did not get her way, or she wouldn't be here talking to Hank. She would be here with her fiancé, celebrating the start of their new life together.

"Here you are, ma'am." The bartender interrupted her train of thought with her shots.

"Oh thank you!" Elaine said, her eyes glistening. This would help take the edge off, she thought to herself.

They each grabbed a shot glass and clinked them together. "To a wonderful vacation!" Hank said.

'To the best vacation ever!!" Elaine said in response, and they clinked their glasses together one more time before tilting their heads back and tossing the harsh liquor down their throats, following the shot with the clamato juice.

Hank made a bit of a face," That wasn't nearly as bad as I thought it was going to be."

Elaine responded with a mock shocked face. "You didn't think that was going to taste good?" she said and then she laughed. "Nobody ever does, but it's amazing, cuts the bitter out right away.

"I imagine not very much could stay bitter around you for very long anyway," Hank said to her, causing her to blush a bit.

Not quite knowing how to react, she looked for something else to say or change the topic to. "OH, look! It's already 4:15! I bet our luggage is in the room, Kristy! Let's go get settled in and ready for dinner. Tonight's a formal dinner remember?" Elaine said as she turned to Kristy.

Kristy had been engrossed in Evan since the moment he had sat down next to her. She was practically in his lap making out with him by now.

"Hmmm, Oh! Yes. I think will finish my drink and meet you in the room if that's okay? Hey... Why don't we all have dinner together?" Kristy suggested.

Elaine was slightly grossed out that her best friend had already attached herself so quickly to another guy for the trip, but decided to make the most of it. At the very least she could have a bit of fun with Evan's brother Hank to amuse her. She had been in worse situations, she thought to herself, smiling.

"That sounds great!" agreed Elaine.

"I'll walk you back to your room?" Hank said.

They left Kristy and Evan at the bar and headed back through the ship toward her suite. They turned down the hall to go to her suite.

"Are you sure that you are going the right way?" Hank asked her. "Pretty sure," replied Elaine. "Why?"

"We must be neighbors then," said Hank. "This is my suite right here. And it looks like they missed some of my luggage. Wonderful," Hank moaned. "Looks like I'll be taking care of this until dinner. I have to get my other bag; it has all of my formal clothing in it. See you at dinner then?"

"Yes, of course. Dinner is fine. I hope they find your bag," Elaine sympathized.

"Me too," Hank replied. "You'll know if they don't because I won't be able to make the dinner. Evan isn't quite my size. Don't worry though, they'll find it," Hank said once more. Elaine wasn't sure if he was trying to reassure her or himself.

Letting herself into her room, she saw her luggage neatly stacked in the center of their suite. She began to put her garments away and settle in, picking out a floor-length black cocktail dress with sparkles across the chest and an asymmetrical neckline for dinner. She began to let her mind wander to Hank; she hoped he did find his bags so that he was able to join them for dinner. Feeling the buzz from the two drinks she had consumed, she lay down for a minute to rest her eyes before dinner.

She awoke a few minutes later hearing her friend's laughter as she made her way toward the suite. Elaine continued to lay on the bed with her eyes closed as she heard Kristy enter the room.

"Come on sleepyhead!! Let's get dressed and go eat dinner!! I'm starving!!" Kristy said loudly.

"Okay, okay, I'm getting up," said Elaine as she sat up and blinked a few times in an attempt to rouse herself.

The girls got dressed in their evening gowns and headed to the main dining room to meet the men for dinner. Hank did manage to show up, having located his garment bag only moments before they were supposed to meet the ladies for dinner. The timing couldn't have been more perfect. The dinner went well, and everyone was happy with the food and service. With full bellies, they decided to continue as a group to check out one of the nightclubs onboard.

Taking their drinks with them, they began to explore their way towards one of the nightclubs; the shops and daytime stores all being closed up gave the boat a bit more of an after-hours feel now. The children and older people who had been roaming the boat earlier were now all tucked away quietly in their rooms, allowing for a more adult ambiance. There were other finely dressed couples quietly walking the boat with their drinks, paused here and there holding each other and looking out over the ocean water as the moon reflected off of the surface.

Finally, they heard the base from the speakers of one of the nightclubs pumping through the hallway. They strategically kept the nightclubs away from the guest suites so that they would never have to worry about complaints of loud music from unwanting patrons.

"This is amazing!" said Kristy, as the group entered into the dimly lit and very loud nightclub. "It feels just like a real nightclub and looks like one too!!"

"It IS amazing! But not as amazing as you!!" Evan said as he picked up Kristy and swung her around in the air. Hank looked down at Elaine and smiled.

"More shots?" he suggested.

"I would love that," Elaine responded back to him.

For the first hour or so Elaine and Hank sat quietly in the corner, nursing their drinks slowly and sharing shots. Before she knew it they had both had 3 shots each. Feeling more adventurous than usual, she decided to try herself on the dance floor. She had never been one to be the center of attention, but she was drunk and on a mission to leave the old Elaine far, far behind, hoping to never ever get hurt the way that she had let her fiancé hurt her.

Now, feeling more than buzzed, Elaine was feeling more adventurous than she had felt in a long time.

"Let's go dance," she said to Hank, grabbing his hand and pulling him onto the dance floor with amazing strength for her size.

Hanks was so shocked that he didn't even have time to protest, he followed behind Elaine's curvy, petite frame and followed her lead as she began to wiggle and grind on his to the beat of the song. He was so entertained by the way her curvy ass felt rubbing against his body, that he didn't care how he looked to other people. He worked his body with her grinding motions, trying to keep himself from growing hard as he worked for his hands around her tiny, wiggling waist.

Elaine turned around and pressed her body close up against Hank's as they continued to move to the music. She pressed her large, round breasts against his stomach and looking up at him with her big round eyes. Hank smiled, and couldn't help but harden slightly upon feeling and seeing the deep valley of cleavage that was pressing against him. He leaned down and kissed Elaine on the lips gently, pulling away quickly so as not to make too much of a public spectacle. Elaine and Hank looked over at Kristy and Evan as they were grinding away on each other, their lips locked as they worked their tongues around in each other's mouths.

Kristy and Evan were doing plenty good enough of a job at making a spectacle out of themselves.

"Shall we go back to your suite or mine?" Hank leaned down and whispered into Elaine's ear. She felt goosebumps run down her back and arms as he nibbled briefly on her ear. Elaine smiled drunkenly and nodded, "Let's go to mine," she said. They grabbed their drinks and began to stumbled their way back to her suite, arm in arm.

"Give me one minute," Hank said as he left her standing for a moment to go tell his brother something. He returned 30 seconds later and smiled at her. "Now we don't have to worry about being interrupted."

"Oh, good idea!" Elaine responded and they headed back toward the suite together.

As soon as they were in her suite, Hank turned her around and pulled her close to his body once more, leaning down and placing his lips onto hers, kissing her deeply. His tongue parted her lips and found its way around the inside of her wet mouth. Elaine felt excited and pressed her tongue back into his mouth, returning the search for the back of his mouth.

She didn't stop him as she felt his hands move around to the back of her dress until they found the top of the zipper and began to work it down. She responded by moving her hands to the top button of his shirt and began to quickly undo each button until she reached the belt holding up his pants. She felt her dress fall to the floor around her and continued to work her hands over Hank's belt, pulling the leather strap out of the buckle and unbuttoning the button at the top of his pants.

She lowered herself to the floor and placed her mouth over the front of his pants, finding the zipper with her tongue, placing it in between her teeth, and pulling it down as she pulled his pants down around his hips with her hands simultaneously.

Hank watched her as she worked on his crotch, his eyes wandering over the lusciousness of her pale curves in the moonlight. Her large breasts were barely contained by the small, strapless bra she had been wearing underneath her evening gown. The black G-string she was wearing disappeared perfectly into the curves of her round ass. Hank's cock began to straighten and harden as he watched her pull his pants down and felt her mouth over the hardness of his flesh through the thin fabric of his boxers.

Elaine worked her thin fingers over the waistband of his boxers and pulled them down as well, Hank's semi-erect cock falling free as she removed the fabric constraint.

Smiling at his size and eager to make him grow all the way for her, Elaine gently held his cock between her soft hands and placed the tip of it between her soft, luscious lips, gently licking at the tip. Smiling up at Hank as she felt the base of his cock flex in between her hands and lips, she sucked harder at the tip and felt him grow fully erect as he let out a low moan of pleasure.

"Mmmmm that's sooo nice," Hank said, and he moved his hands onto her head, his fingers working through her fine hair as he pulled her head farther onto his stiff cock, pressing the tip of it into the back of Elaine's throat causing her to gag a bit. He released the force on her head as she gagged, and allowed her to move her head back and breathe.

"Sorry about that baby," Hank said. "Let's make you more comfortable."

He took her hand and pulled her up to her feet, leading her over to the bed, their clothing left in piles on the floor. His shirt still hung on his frame, and he pulled his arms out of it as he smiled at Elaine. Looking like a vision of sex, lying almost naked on the white bedspread. Hank climbed on the bed and straddled her. He bent down and gave her a brief kiss on the lips before moving down to her breasts.

Taking one in each hand, Hank gently massaged them as he went back and forth between her nipples, flicking at them with his tongue and the nibbling them gently as the little pink buttons hardened in his mouth. Elaine felt the dampness on her panties grow while her nipples hardened in Hank's mouth, and she moved her hips, pressing her wetness into his body with a soft, gentle rhythm.

"Not yet," he said to her, smiling and he removed her thong slowly and deliberately, looking at the beautiful pink wetness that glistened at him from in between her pale thighs. He moved his head down and lay it gently on the inside of her thigh as his tongue slowly licked up and down the length of her slit, tasting her sweet moisture as he lapped at her wet, pink lips. Finding the top of her clit he began to work his tongue over the top of it, flicking it back and forth quickly as he sent her body into little convulsions. Elaine worked to keep her moaning down to a minimum, not knowing how thin the walls were between suites.

Running her fingers through Hank's tousled hair as he slipped two fingers into her soaking wet pussy while he continued to lick at her clit, Elaine let out a small scream of pleasure and pulled his head into her farther. Grinding her hips against his face, Elaine closed her eyes and laid her head back as once again the waves of pleasure flooded her body with his tongue flicking back and forth on her clit. He began to work one finger in and out of her tight, wet hole in search of her G-spot, pressing his finger further and further back into her until he found what he was looking for. Elaine's body jolted and spasmed as she worked to control her moans and screams so that they did not escape the conference room. Hank looked up at her and smiled as he sucked on the fluids that were now gushing out of her body uncontrollably, squirting into his mouth.

"Oh, God Hank... Oh, I want more!" Elaine managed to get out, as she came all over Hank's face.

Hank lapped at her wet hole as her cum came pulsing out all over his face, her legs quivering and thighs shaking as they pressed against his head. He didn't stop sucking and lapping at her until she had finished and began to relax her legs a bit.

"Mmmm oh you are definitely going to be getting more. Right about.... Now...." Hank said to her with a devious smile as he sat up and positioned the tip of his cock in between her pussy lips. Placing his hands firmly on her hips, he knew that she was tight but decided to force himself into her with one solid thrust.

. . .

She stifled a scream as she felt him slowly push his thick member in between her pink lips, and let out a gasp as he slid his entire length deep into her hole. He grabbed her hips and pumped himself in and out of her, slowly at first as she loosened up with the motion. Pounding harder and harder as her tits bounced back and forth, Hank relished the tightness of her pussy as it squeezed over his thick, hard member. She moaned as he thrust harder and harder in and out of her tight hole over and over again, feeling her tighten around his cock as once again he was causing her to cum and squirt uncontrollably on him.

Hank held himself inside of her until her pulsing slowed once more.

"Not quite done with you yet," Hank said to her as he pulled his long, wet rod out from in between her soaked thighs. He rolled over onto his back and pulled Elaine on top of his lap, her legs and pussy straddled over his erect cock.

"Mmmmmm I hope not..."

His hand placed firmly on her hips, he guided her down onto the hardness of his thick shaft. Both of them moaned softly in pleasure as they felt the sensation of being inside of one another, filling them both with ecstasy. Elaine worked her hips on his lap, grinding her tight, wet pussy hard and deep down the length of his shaft, feeling the shivers of excitement as they passed through them both.

Hank licked and bit at the hard nipples of her large breasts as they bounced in front of his face, feeling his cock throb harder and harder inside her tight wet pussy as it slapped up and down on his lap. Elaine ground her nails into her shoulders as her legs began to tremble in anticipation of the cum that was about to be released. She let out a scream as her legs trembled, her cum once again squirting and pulsing out of her, this time Hank's large shaft responding and releasing as his hot cum shot up inside of her simultaneously. Hank couldn't contain his pleasure and let out a low moan as Elaine stifled her own screams. They held each other tightly as they came together, pulsing in unison, their creamy fluids mixing as they dripped out of Elaine's hole over Hank's softening member. Elaine pulled herself off of Hank's cock and lay next to him. Both drunk and exhausted from their tryst, they passed out.

The morning arrived and Elaine woke up to find her partner still passed out naked next to her. Looking out the window, she squinted as her eyes adjusted to the brightness of the morning sun. She looked out over the still waters and looked at the birds flying in the air. Hank stirred next to her and sat up looking out the window, blinking as the wheels in his head slowly turned.

"Birds?" Hank said randomly.

"Yea, what's wrong with birds?" Elaine asked.

"Well, I thought we weren't supposed to be at our first port until tomorrow?" Hank asked.

"That's what the schedule says," Elaine responded.

"Well, you don't see birds like that when you're moving at sea. You see birds like that when you are docked," Hank explained as he got out of bed and began to retrieve his clothing from the pile on the floor.

"I'm going to see if I can get back into my room, change clothes and go find out what's been going on," Hank said as he put on his pants. Just then they heard a knocking on the suite door.

"Elaine? It's Kristy, can I come back yet?" Kristy asked in a muffled voice through the door.

"Yes, of course. Come on in," Elaine said loudly enough for Kristy to hear her through the door. She grabbed a shirt out of one of the drawers next to the bed and slipped it on over her naked body just as Kristy and Evan made their way in through the front door.

"I'll be seeing you later I hope?" Hank said as he slipped out past Kristy on her way in.

"Did you hear what was wrong with the boat?" Kristy asked, making sure the door was closed tightly behind her.

"Something's wrong with the ship?" Elaine responded in a concerned tone of voice. "I didn't hear anything about that. Hank had said something about finding out why we were at Port. That's what he was on his way out the door to go do.

What did you hear?"

"Well, Evan and I got up this morning to go have breakfast and noticed that we were docked. So we asked our waiter what the deal was and apparently, one of the main engines messed up last night, so now we're stuck in at the Grand Caymans while they get it repaired. We're going to be here for at least one night they say," Kristy informed her.

"Wow. That's crazy. At least we're all okay and not stuck out at sea. Why don't we get dressed and go check out the island? I still haven't eaten, but I'm sure I can find something to eat once we get down there. It'll be nice to get some real land under my feet anyway," Elaine said positively, happy to have Hank gone and to be focusing on her girl's trip once more. Sure, she had a good time last night with him, but he wasn't what she was looking for or longing for and she wasn't even sure if she wanted to sleep with him again. As good as he was, she was still looking for something else, another connection that would bind her more tightly to a person. She didn't know exactly what it was, but she would know it when she found it.

The girls got dressed and headed out and off of the big

ship. Wearing long, light cotton maxi dresses and big-brimmed straw sunhats, they both looked suave and elegant as they glided down the ramp and onto the pier. Breathing in deep through her nose, she relished the sweet salty air and could smell something good frying in the distance. Her tummy growled quietly letting her know the first priority while they were making the most of their stop.

"Something smells delicious and we are going to go find that first!" Elaine said and began to head in the direction of the delicious smell with Kristy right beside her. They came upon a small café overlooking the bay and the giant ship they had just came off of.

"Upstairs or down?" the maître d' asked the two ladies.

"Upstairs please, on the balcony," Kristy requested.

They followed their host upstairs and were seated at a small table on the tiny terrace backing up next to another small table, which was also blessed with the same beautiful and airy location. Seated at the table were two extremely handsome men dressed in designer linen pants, with expensive boat shoes and lightweight t-shirts. Elaine felt goosebumps of excitement run down her arms as the older of the two gentlemen looked up from his menu and smiled at her. His piercing green eyes seemed to stare right through her soul, and she felt the excitement rise in her cheeks and looked away quickly.

"Here you are ladies, your server will be right with you," said the maître d' leaving the ladies on the balcony.

Elaine did her best to stay focused on ordering food and talking to Kristy, doing her best to avoid being distracted by the presence of the sexy, mysterious man at the table next to them. Eventually, Kristy excused herself to go to the bathroom, leaving Elaine to fend for herself at the table. It was all she could do to not just stare at the man next to her.

Something about him, his looks, his clothing, maybe it was the calm, quiet, and yet strong energy that he seemed to exude.

"I don't want to be nosey or rude. But I saw that you and your friend walked over here from the cruise ship," the handsome stranger at the table next to her interrupted her thoughts. Startled she attempted to recover smoothly.

"I, uh, yes we did," Elaine stammered out, drawn in by the intensity in his eyes.

"I overheard that you were to be stuck in port for a couple of nights I would like to extend an invitation to you to show you two ladies around the island. Being a local, I know all of the best spots. And we can go in my air-conditioned hummer as opposed to you and your poor friend suffering in an unairconditioned tour bus on this horribly hot island. It would be my pleasure," he said to her with sincerity and kindness in his eyes.

Her heart skipped a beat. It was almost as if he could read her mind.

"I'd love that," Elaine said to him. "I will of course need to check with my friend when she gets back but I don't see why she would say no. My name is Elaine."

"My name is Chad," he said smiling at her, extending his hand to shake hers.

CHAPTER 2

ELAINE SHOOK CHAD'S HAND, happily surprised at the strength with which he gripped her own. His eyes gazed fiercely and deeply into her own as he smiled and let go.

"It's a pleasure to meet you," said Elaine, not knowing why her heart was pounding so wildly but so excited by this his presence.

"So how exactly do you know so much about this place?" she asked Chad.

"Other than owning most of the bloody thing I've lived here for about 10 years now. I got sick of my parents in my first year of high school. They wanted to send me to a boarding school, but instead, I came here, and using the internet to fuel my funds they allowed me to stay so long as I was profitable. So here I am," Chad said with a smile.

"It might sound a bit pompous, but that's my story. Once your friend gets back let's hop in my whip and we will go cruise around. I know an excellent tubing spot as well as the best place to watch the sunset on the whole island," Chad said, still smiling at her.

He was intrigued by her simple beauty and her quiet,

broken air she exuded. It was as though she was a hailed-on flower trying to recoup from the terrible storm. Chad was always drawn to the more emotionally weak girls, they often allowed him to go much further with them in terms of physical limits and emotional. Their need to please was always so outrageously high, which was something that he got off on tremendously.

Kristy walked back from the bathroom. "Who's your new friend?" she asked jokingly.

"This is Chad," said Elaine excitedly, "He offered to show us around the island!"

Kristy looked a bit skeptical, but saw the excitement in her friend's face and let her skepticism slide, and decided to roll with the day. The ship was already busted, what else could go wrong.

"Hi, I'm Chad, and this is my friend Kyle."

Elaine and Kristy followed Chad out of the restaurant and down the stairs. The valet had brought Chad's car around and had it waiting for them with the convertible top down. Kristy's mouth dropped open as she looked over the vintage convertible Bentley in its perfect condition. The perfect black paint and shining Chrome pieces sparkling in the sun. The air conditioning was blasting despite the windows and top being down and the girls slid onto the cool leather seats.

"Oh my god! This car is fabulous!" Kristy cooed. Elaine couldn't agree more, but didn't say anything, she just smiled at Chad as he slid into the driver's seat.

"Sorry if you ladies are a little squashed back there. The model isn't exactly known for its roominess." Chad said in a svelte voice as the car cruised away from the restaurant by the pier.

"I'll drive you ladies through town and then you can tell

me if you'd rather I take you to my favorite beach or my favorite caves and we can top that off with dinner and watching the sunset, yes ladies?" Chad half asked half told them.

"As long as we are back at the boat with eight like they requested, that is fine by me," Kristy approved.

"I could care less if I ever go back, " Elaine said, loving the sea breeze in her hair as they cruised down the tropical main street, with its Street market and various vendors set up selling everything from rum to Airbrushed t-shirts and in between.

"Let's head to the caves, then, it's the best of both worlds," Chad insisted.

The girls watched out the window as the small city of George Town slip past them with its pristine pastel-colored houses lined out in neat little rows. Chad turned on the stereo blasting some old Johnny Cash as they cruised down the small island highway, the salty sea air blowing in their hair. Elaine felt like she was in a dream, with a beautiful island to explore, a gorgeous and very sexy tour guide, and riding around in a car that was worth more than all of the houses she lived in combined.

Chad turned off the highway and onto a small sandy road winding their way through a small wooded area until they came to a clearing with a neat little cabin. He parked the Bentley next to the cabin and everyone piled out of the car. Walking over to the cabin and unlocking the front door, he held it open as he ushered everyone in.

"Ladies, come on in. This is one of my favorite little spots on the island. I'm going to get changed into some swim trunks. If you ladies would like to get changed, there's a changing room through that door. There should be some swimsuits in there that are your size if you didn't bring yours with you," Chad said as he walked off through a beautifully hand-carved oak door into another room and closed it behind him.

"I'm going to go change in here ladies. See you shortly," Kyle said as he disappeared behind another door.

The ladies looked at one another and tried not to look too shocked by how lavish the little cabin was on the inside. It hadn't looked that big from the outside. The walls were paneled with light-colored natural wood and there were beautiful rugs laid all around amidst the 3 lounges and two overstuffed chairs that took up the main area of the little cabin. They wandered through the door that Chad had directed them toward and found a room even larger than they had imagined. It had been designed for the sole purpose of being a women's changing room and had a variety of hooks all over the walls for hanging towels and swimsuits. There were large floor-to-ceiling mirrors with beautifully beveled edges and benches here and there. There were a couple of doors within the room and after closing the main door behind them the girls opened the others to find out what was behind them. Behind Elaine's door was a lavish bathroom, with a sparse but elegant shower, sink and toilet. Kristy let out a gasp as she opened her door. Inside the closet hung numerous designer swimsuits in various sizes and styles, brand new with the tags on them still.

"Who is this guy?!" Kristy exclaimed!

"I have no idea, but I plan on finding out," Elaine said, walking across the room to look through the closet with Kristy.

"Wow, this stuff is awesome! Look at some of these suits!! We have to try some on. I've never even thought about trying on suits this expensive before. I've wanted to but I... well you know," Elaine said, laughing as she pulled a couple of suits out of the closet to try on.

"I wonder what's in this," Elaine asked, bending down to look more closely at an ornately carved wooden trunk that was tucked into the back corner of the closet. Picking at the lock she tried to pull it open, but it wouldn't budge.

"Must not be for us then," Kristy said as she pulled a couple of suits for her to try on.

"Hmm, must not be," Elaine replied, curious as to what on earth he could possibly be keeping in a fancy locked trunk in his women's changing room of this random cabin.

The girls tried on swimsuits until they found ones that they loved and went out into the main room to see what Chad had in store for them. They found Chad and Kyle sitting in the room with four giant inflatable black inner tubes, grinning at them mischievously.

"Hope you girls like a bit of adventure. You both know how to swim right?" Chad asked.

"Of course we do. That would be dumb. To go on a cruise if you didn't even know how to swim. Why would you go on a boat at all?" Kristy commented in a slightly irritated tone of voice.

Elaine could almost see Chad as cringed from the sound of her voice.

"Okay, well," he said almost firmly," Then this is going to be a super fun time!" His tone of voice lightened up at the end of his sentence and he grabbed a tube and handed it to Elaine. Kyle handed a tube to Kristy. "For you my lady," he said.

"Thank you," she replied.

"For the queen bee," Chad said, winking to Elaine.

She could feel herself begin to blush as she took the tube from Chad's hands, brushing her fingers over his as she pulled it from his grip. His eyes caught with hers and his smile grew bigger at the feel of her skin on his, Elaine felt sparks that she hadn't felt in a long time... if ever.

"Follow me now. We have a little bit of a hike, but not much," Chad said. The crew followed him out of the little cabin and down a path through the tropical forest. They walked down the path for about seven minutes listening to the roar of the water grow louder and louder.

"There's a waterfall up here, but don't worry, we are getting in at the bottom of it," Chad said to Elaine.

"It's actually quite tame. You'll love it. It's peaceful and beautiful and the best is at the very end, but I won't ruin the surprise for you," Chad told her as they approached the top of a small hill.

Once they reached the top of the small hill the rushing water they had been hearing came into view. The gorgeous crystal clear river was flowing beautifully with the rushing waterfall in the background. The lush foliage and beautiful tropical flowers all around made it feel like an image out of a travel magazine. There were even large black iguanas sunning themselves. The water from the fall flowed over a high rocky cliff embedded with outcroppings of hanging moss and more bright flowers and the water pooled at the bottom and ran through the woods for a bit before disappearing into the dark mouth of a large cave.

"This is gorgeous!!" Elaine said under her breath, taking in the pristine scene before her. It was almost as though it had never been touched by other humans.

"Wow! This really is amazing! What do you have like the best of everything?" Kristy exclaimed.

"Oh, not quite yet, but I definitely know the best of everything," Chad said knowingly as he looked Elaine in the eyes. Elaine felt her heart flutter as he seemed to stare deep into her soul. Chad looked away and walked to the water's edge. He took off his flip-flops and dipped his foot into the water. "Ah, perfect," he said. He picked up his flip-flops and walked over to a stump next to a tree on the river bank and opened up the top much to Kristy and Elaine's astonishment and tossed his shoes inside.

"I kind of come here a lot," Chad said having noticed the shocked look on the girls' faces. Kyle was taking off his shoes and putting them in the tree trunk like normal, so Kristy and Elaine followed suit. Elaine felt the cool, clean water rush against her legs as she walked down the

Testing the water they all cautiously got in the tubes and slowly eased into the water.

"Just lay back and relax, it's a super tame ride and you'll love where we come out at. Should take about an hour," Chad said as he pulled his legs up onto his tube and let the current carry him away down the stream and towards the dark opening of the cave.

Kyle followed right behind him after letting out a, "woo hoo". Elaine and Kristy looked at each other, smiled, and pulled their feet up off the smooth rocks on the bottom of the shallow river bed and let themselves be carried away by the current. Following closely behind Kyle and Chad the girls entered into the cave as the light began to grow dim. The light became so dark that they couldn't even see each other for about a minute before it began to lighten up again as they exited the cave coming out into a less densely forested area with light sandy soil and palm trees interspersed here and there.

Elaine relaxed and lay back looking up at the light blue sky above them and feeling the cool water as it carried her away downstream. She floated for what felt like an eternity and was a bit surprised when she felt her tube being bumped by something. Opening her eyes, she saw that Chad had managed to slow himself down so that he was right next to her now.

"Hold my hand," he insisted. "The next cave is a little long and dark and there are a couple of spots where the water whirlpools and you can be stuck for a while if you don't know where you are going."

"Yes, sir," Elaine said with a smile and she reached her hand over her tube and grabbed onto Chad's outstretched hand. She looked ahead and realized they were about to enter one last tunnel. Chad squeezed her hand and she squeezed back, feeling her heart flutter and loving the strength and size of his hand compared to her own. The light left them once more and she was grateful to have his hand on her own. It made her feel safe and warm in the dark cave. It was almost as if they were floating through the night, the cool sea breeze blowing the cave across their bodies. She relaxed as she felt Chad's fingers run up and down her hand as he held it tight and longed to feel him run his fingers on other parts of her body. The current began to pick up and she tightened her grip suddenly. Feeling her tense up Chad pulled her tube next to his own and felt him begin to kick with his legs through the current.

"This is where one of the whirlpools is. We'll be right past in a minute. Just hold on to me," Chad instructed.

Elaine tensed up a bit more and gripped the other side of her tube tighter. Not wanting to grab onto him too hard and look like a wimp. The current increased and she felt it begin to pull her tube in. Chad gave two big kicks and pushed them right past the swirling eddies and back into the main current. As the waters slowed again and she loosened her grip on Chad's hand.

"Don't let go quite yet. One more right around the corner," Chad instructed.

She tightened her grip as she felt the begin the process again. She heard Kristy and Kyle holler with excitement as they rolled through it first. And then giggled as they rolled through it together. The cave began to grow light as they neared the other end of it and she began to hear breakers. It was almost impossible to be able to really see anything for a minute after they floated out of the pitch black, back into the bright light of the sun. Once her eyes adjusted she gasped at the beauty of the lagoon which they had been poured out into. Looking up behind her, she saw the big cliff which contained the cave they had just floated through. The white sandy beaches and palm trees scattered about were almost too much for Elaine.

"Yup, I never want to leave," she said matter of factly.

"You don't have to. I didn't," Chad said, looking at her with a knowing smile.

"Let's get out and grab a bite to eat on the boat. What do you say?" Chad said as he let go of Elaine's hand and began to paddle his tube toward the white sandy beach.

"You have a boat here too? What don't you have?!" Kristy said as they made their way onto the shore. "I don't have an amazing woman," Chad said looking at Elaine.

Elaine turned a bright red and Kristy laughed.

Chad walked over to another tree truck similar to the one that had been at the beginning of their journey and grabbed out another pair of flip slops and tossed a pair over to Kyle.

"Sorry ladies. I don't have any for you here. I wasn't exactly planning your being with us today. I will have Jose bring over all of your things while we are on the boat. You won't need anything but your swimsuit on there anyway.

It's not a long walk though and it's mostly sand so you should both be fine," Chad said as he began to walk down the path.

The group walked through the beachy lagoon forest for only a few moments. Hearing the breakers and seeing the ocean open up before them as the palm trees came to an end. They looked down the beach and saw a long pier which went out to a large white yacht. Walking up to the large boat the girls realized that it was already on and running.

"I got it about 2 years ago. Top of the line. Probably spent way too much money on it. But I love it. It only holds 14 but there's room for 40 staff members," Chad said very simply as though everyone had one.

"You have 40 staff members on there?" Elaine asked incredulously.

"Ha! No, maybe if I was going to go all the way to the States in it or something like that. But I almost always take the jet when I have to go away from the island. No, right now there should be four staff on. Two running the ship, one in the kitchen and my butler. He's great at staying out of the way though.

They all are really, so no need to worry about feeling weird or anything," Chad told Elaine.

Elaine smiled to herself. If this was his boat she was excited to see what his house was like. And what other amazing things he had in store for her. They walked across the sandy beach and down the skinny wooden pier to the large yacht. Neither Elaine nor Kristy had ever been on a boat of this caliber and were amazed by the amenities once they were on board.

Following Chad onto the boat, they entered through the cargo hold which was level with the pier and walked through the pristine and meticulously organized lower hold and up a thin staircase it opened up onto the sprawling deck. There was a clear blue pool in the shape of different size circles connecting together with the smallest circle at the top being contained as a hot tub. Walking around the pool at the deep end was contained by a 6-foot-tall clear wall, allowing the viewers to easily see what was happening within the water of the pool.

Walking past the pool and hot tub they came to some large square lounges and tables underneath the upper deck of the yacht and on the same upper level as the hot tub. There was a little bar in the corner, fully stocked, and a small chrome grilling area. Beyond the wall were two staircases leading onto the upper two decks of the yacht.

Chad was right about the girls not noticing his staff. Or perhaps it was because they were too busy taking in the regal furniture of the lavish boat.

The girls lounged on the furniture with their glasses of wine as they wait for the men to come back out. Enjoying the breeze from the wind in their hair as the boat began to pull away from the small pier and secluded beach.

"I'm so glad that you agreed to come," Kristy said as she raised her wine glass up in the air. "Cheers!" Kristy said.

"To new adventures!!" Elaine said as she raised her glass and clicked it with Kristy's. After finishing her swallow, she got up from the lounge chair and walked over to the hot tub and pool. Testing the hot tub water, she found that it was very hot, too hot for during a hot day in the sun. She walked over to one of the deeper circles and placed her hand inside feeling the cool water rush over her fingers. Feeling hot and sweaty still, she looked at Kristy and smiled.

"I'm getting in. Want to join me?" Elaine asked.

"No, I'm good. Thank you. I'm going to lie here in the shade and enjoy my wine," Kristy said.

Elaine climbed into the pool with her glass of wine being careful not to spill a drop. Lowering her body into the cool water she instantly felt more refreshed. She put the glass to her lips again and felt the cool white wine as it poured down her throat.

Closing her eyes and laying back and floating in the water while she still held her glass upright she relished every lavish moment. This was far too good to be true. Almost like a dream come true. She let her eyes wander over the plush deck and bar area and noticed and small chest tucked away high on a shelf that was almost identical to the one which had been in the closet at the beginning of their tubing journey. Maybe it was some sort of emergency preparedness kit she thought to herself. But then why would it be locked. Everything else about him was so open and available to those he had around him.

Perhaps she could get him to show her what was in the box a bit later one. Maybe after a few drinks, she thought to herself.

Chad and Kyle walked down one of the narrow stair-cases in fresh swim trucks and light robes tossed over each one. Chad was carrying a fresh bottle of champagne to crack open.

"OH champagne!!" Kristy crooned.

"I figured we could have ourselves a little toast to this beautiful day and our new friendship," Chad said with a smile. Kyle set down the 4 crystal champagne glasses that he had been carrying on the smooth bar top. Chad popped open the Champagne, sending the cork flying over the side of the yacht.

"Whoa!" he exclaimed as the bubbly liquid flowed out

of the bottle. He quickly moved it so that the stream of bubbles was falling into the glasses on the bar. Having filled the glasses, he handed on one to Kyle and one to Kristy. Taking one for himself, he walked all the way around the pool. Looking through the glass side at Elaine's long body as she swam languidly in the cool water. The smooth curves of her breasts and ass exciting him through the form-fitting bikini she had chosen to wear. Walking over to the deepest part and walking up the stairs on the side of the pool until he reached the top.

"You're going to have to swim over here to get this," he said with a joking smile.

"Making me work so hard," Elaine joked back with him as she began to kick and paddle towards him. "Backstroke..." Chad said.

"Huh? " Elaine asked, confirming the odd request.

"You know how to swim, I think that you should have to backstroke over now. You know. Just to help you overcome your lazy streak," Chad said. "That is of course if you really want your glass of champagne."

"Oh, I see how you are going to be," said Elaine as she rolled over onto her back and began to move her arms and legs, gliding through the water towards Chad. She was turned on and excited by the way that he told her what to do. Looking at him and smiling the whole way she watched his eyes as they moved up and down the length of her body. Pausing as he stared at her large breasts and once more at her smooth thighs and hips. She felt excited and wanted to let him see more of her. She wanted him to undress her with his hands and his mouth, not just his eyes. Reaching the far end of the pool where Chad sat she pulled herself out with the help of his firm hand. They raised their glasses in the air as Chad said a brief toast praising the glorious day and the adventures with both of their friends.

Elaine tossed back her head and let the cold bubbles wash down her throat and handed the empty champagne glass to Chad.

"Thirsty girl," he said with a smile as he took the empty glass from her hand.

He tipped his head back and finished the second half of his drink in the next gulp and smiled and set his glass down next to her empty one. He then reached and took her wine glass out of her hand and set it down next to the empty champagne glasses.

"Hey, I'm not done with that---"Elaine was cut short as Chad grabbed her swiftly by the shoulders and threw her back into the pool. He dove in after her, coming up behind her with his strong arms and pulling her close to his warm body in the cool water.

"Now, you can have it back," Chad said with a smile as he reached over to her glass and handed it to her.

Elaine looked over worried that maybe Kristy and Kyle weren't having a good time, but lost her worries when she realized that they were snuggling happily on the large lounge chair underneath a giant plush white towel blanket and were happily talking to each other as they sipped on their drinks. Kyle pointed to the shoreline every now and again as they passed a different landmark.

"Don't worry about them. They'll be just fine," Chad said to her. Elaine smiled at him as she took another sip of her wine, feeling the warmth of the alcohol and feeling a buzz from the glass of champagne she had drank a bit too quickly. She leaned back into his arms once more, feeling his broad chest pressing up against her own petite back. She felt his soft lump of manhood as it pressed against her ass through the wet fabric of his swim trunks and felt her pussy lips tingle and goosebumps ran down her arms.

"Mmmmmm, are you chilly, Here turn this way. And take another big drink of your wine," Chad said as he tipped the cup that was in her hand back up against her mouth, forcing her head back gently. She parted her lips as she let him pour the liquid into her mouth. It was seductive, the way that he was so in charge of her. He took the glass away and set it back on the edge of the pool and then spun her body around pulling her closer into him. He wrapped his arms around her and rubbed his hands up and down her back to warm her up and bit. She pressed her large breasts against his warm chest and wrapped her leg and around his waist as she let his warmth spread to her. He walked backward leaning up against the edge of the pool wall and she reached for her wine glass behind his head.

Chad began to work his hands up and down her back as she put the glass to her lips for another sip. He placed his thick, soft lips against her smooth neck as she gulped down more wine.

"Very thirsty girl, aren't you?" Chad said as he ran his hands over her ass and pulled her pussy down onto his crotch.

"Hm, not too thirsty," Elaine said a bit defensively. "I am on vacation."

"Oh, I'm not judging. I just think we are going to need to get you something more satisfying to sip on soon," Chad said to her, nibbling on her ear lobe and sending chills down her arms once more.

"Shall we move to the hot tub," he suggested.

"Actually, I'm going to need to go to the little girls' room soon," Elaine said.

"Oh, of course. I should have shown it to you when you

arrived on the boat. I'll take you up to the bathroom in my room. I think I even have some clothes that might work for you up there still," Chad picked her up and set her on the edge of the pool, and lifted himself out next to her. Helping her up and handing her a fluffy towel from a nearby rack, he wrapped it gently around her wet body.

Elaine followed Chad's dripping wet body across the deck and up one of the narrow flights of stairs. He opened the small door at the top of the stairs and she shivered again, feeling the blast of air-conditioned air as it poured out of the upper deck onto them.

"Oh, brrr, that's a bit chilly," Elaine said.

"Don't worry beautiful. We will get you all fixed up so that you are perfectly comfortable. I can turn the AC down in here too," Chad said, smiling as she walked up the top of the stairs past him and into the immaculately designed master bedroom of the yacht.

"Although I'm not sure that I want to," he said, looking down at her hard nipples.

Its open floor plan had a large California king bed with white sheets and bedspread and pillows in the middle. With expensive mirrored furniture with exquisite beveled edges. The fully mirrored armoire standing behind the bed and another nightstand as well and a tea cart which held on it the necessities for a quick nightcap.

"Bathroom is over that way," Chad told her pointing to a door on the far side of the room. She let herself into the bathroom and fuzzily made her way to the toilet to pee. Sitting on the toilet, she began to realize how fuzzy she was getting and talked herself into slowing down the drinks a bit. She pulled the gold knob on the top of the ivory tank to flush the fancy toilet and washed her hands in the white marble sink with matching gold faucets.

Walking back out onto the bedroom, she saw Chad laying sprawled out on the bed.

"Come over here and lay with me for a minute. It's a beautiful view from up here anyway. Half of the room was floor-to-ceiling length windows which opened up on both sides and the front so that the persons inside could see the gorgeous landscape or waterscape which surrounded them. She noticed another little chest tucked away underneath the corner of his bed. What was with all of these chests he had everywhere? There had to be something to them. Not feeling it quite appropriate to ask about the yet she obeyed him and walked over to the bed. Climbing up on top of it and laying down next to Chad as they looked out the window together.

He reached over and pulled her head close to him forcefully, parting her lips with his tongue and shoving it down with surprising force. She almost pulled back, she was so taken aback by his strength, but she fell further into it instead. Searching into the wet depths of his mouth with her own tongue. Chad rolled over onto his back and pulled Elaine on top of him so that her legs were straddling over his waist. He was still soft beneath her but she could feel him underneath her pussy regardless and longed to feel his member grow hard.

He pulled her once again down to his face and kissed her deeply before grabbing her hair and making a ponytail in his hand, he forced her head down to the crotch of his wet swim trunks.

"Why don't you try to quench your thirst with this," Chad said, not letting go of her hair.

She parted her lips and softly kissed the damp fabric over his soft man parts. She moved her hands to the side of his swim trunks and pulled them down over his hips, his soft cock laying there, waiting for her to bring it to life.

Chad relaxed his grip on her hair but didn't completely let go as she began to work her wet tongue over the soft flesh of his cock. She felt herself grow warm and damp between her legs with excitement. She had never had a man be this direct and forceful with her before. And she wanted every bit of what he had in store for her.

Taking her hands and lifting his member into her mouth, she began to suck on the soft tip of his head. Using her hair Chad began to pump Elaine's head up and down, ever so slowly and gently. He began to push her head farther and farther down on his soft member until Elaine pushed back against his head to pull back and breathe for a second. She felt his cock flinch and grow harder as she took a moment and then went back down on him.

He pressed her head down quickly causing her to choke on his semi-erect member. She choked a bit on him and felt him solidify in her mouth, growing longer and wider inside of her. She choked again and he released her head a bit, allowing her to get a full breath again before she continued to work her wet mouth over his hard cock.

"You are a thirsty girl. Don't let me get too rough with you. I kind of like it a bit harder than most," Chad said to her with a mysterious smirk. Pushing her head down on his cock once again, she looked up at him with smiling eyes and pulled her mouth off of his cock as he allowed her to come up for a deep breath of air.

"I think I can handle it," Elaine said with a smile.

"Now that's a good girl," Chad said as she worked up and down on his cock with more intensity. She began to stuff his cock down her own throat with such fervor that he let go of her hair and placed his hands behind his head as he gazed down at her lustfully.

This continued for a few moments before she began to feel him go a bit softer. Before she could do anything about it, he grabbed her by the arms and flipped her over so that he was on top of her now.

"Such a good girl, I think you deserve to be treated back a little. If I may?" Chad asked as he kissed down the deep v of her cleavage and bit on her nipples through the fabric of her bikini top.

"Oh yes, please," Elaine almost begged as she ground her pussy up into his crotch, not being able to move very much by the way he was pinning her down in between his thighs.

"Just lay there and hold still," Chad said as he pulled on the stings of her bikini top until they were undone, pulled the small piece of fabric off of her chest, and threw it to the floor beside the bed. He looked down at her beautiful naked breasts and she lay excited underneath him. Awaiting the pleasure he was about to inflict upon her body, her nipples hardened with anticipation and he leaned down to lick and kiss them gently. Suddenly she felt his teeth bite down hard on her right nipple and she let out a scream and tried to squirm out of reflex to get away from the sharp little bite.

"Mmmmmm, I said hold still," Chad said firmly as he grabbed both of her arms and pinned them down firmly to the bed beneath her.

"Stay," he said even more firmly as he released her arms and moved as he quickly slid off her bikini bottoms revealing her damp, shiny pussy lips.

Placing his hands firmly on her thighs, he lowered his head to her clit and began to lick the tiny button with the tip of his tongue. Elaine instantly wiggled a jerked from the incredible sensations that he was sending through her body with each flick of his tongue. The more that she wiggle the more firmly that he held her thighs to the bed in an attempt to keep her still. Once she had escaped him as her leg flung free of his hand while his tongue danced on her clit.

"I am going to make you hold still if you aren't going to do it on your own," Chad said threatening.

"I'll give you one more chance," he whispered as he placed his head once again between her wet thighs. This time sliding finger into her wet hole as his tongue worked up and down her slits. She screamed and her body flinched tremendously as his finger found her g-spot.

"That's it," Chad said, pulling his head out from between her thighs. He leaned up towards her head and she thought for a moment that he was going to kiss her, but he continued over her, reaching over the bed and grabbing something, she felt him slip a soft cloth over her hand and tighten it onto her wrist.

Moving quickly he did the same to her other wrist and getting off of the bed, took his time walking around to softly restrain her legs.

"I want you to know I would never do anything to hurt you. This is only so that you will hold still for me. Let me know if anything becomes too much for you please," Chad said somewhat drunkenly.

He climbed back onto the bed and once again returned to licking on the delicious, pink folds in between her thighs. She tried to squirm and move, but she couldn't, held down to the bed with the soft restraints. Only little movements of her hips and he easily kept up with those. Sucking and lapping at her clit and up and down the length of her lips he continued to build her up, almost until she felt like she couldn't take it anymore. Her thighs began to shake and her pussy began to throb on his fingers as she felt herself begin to cum on him. Feeling this he quickly pulled himself away from her thighs and his fingers out of her wet hole and she slowed the cumming she had almost started.

"Not quite yet," Chad said with another mischievous look in his eyes.

He mounted himself over her, his cock once again rock hard as he looked at her petite body tied down tightly to his bed. Not able to escape from him, not that she would want to. She wanted him to slide his huge, thick unit in between her legs so badly.

"Get me wet for you," Chad said as he dangled his cock over her mouth. She licked and sucked on his cock leaving as much saliva as she could and he moved his hips down until he was lined up with her pelvis. Grabbing her by the waist Chad slowly slipped the tip of his fat cock in between her lips. Playing with her wetness and dipping it slowly in and out of her hole as she tried to grind her pelvis into him, longing to feel his hard shaft penetrate deeply into her.

Looking down at her as she tried to push her pussy father onto his cock from her restrained state she smiled lovingly at her.

"So thirsty for that cock pretty girl," and he thrust himself hard and deep into her. She let out a loud scream as he penetrated further into her body than she had ever felt a man's cock go before. He continued to thrust his shaft in and out of her while she lay on the bed, letting out a scream of pleasure with each hard stroke.

He reached down and placed his fingers in her hair, gripping it roughly, and began to thrust himself into her with more intensity.

Elaine had never been fucked with such veracity before, but she loved every minute of his hard, pounding cock deep inside of her. Growing wetter and wetter until her legs and thighs gave way to trembling as she came all over his hard cock. She felt his cock begin to throb, but then he pulled back so that the tip was barely inside of her as she squirted her hot cum around his head with a force she had never felt before. She began to let out a large scream and he clamped his hand down over her mouth, muffling the sound that she was unable to control coming out of her mouth.

"We do have company you know," he said to her and he began to pound his cock inside of her again, voraciously with his hand over her mouth to trap her loud screaming inside of her. She had thought that she could take no more but was in no position to resist his powerful motions, she lay and took his pounding as his hands gripped her head more intensely, his fingernail pressing into her skull as she began to feel his large cock throb hard inside of her soaked pussy. She bit his hand so that she could scream as he had brought her to a precipice once more. Pulling away, she felt his cock throb even harder and he raised his hand, pulling it back. Slapping her hard across her face with the back of it as his hot cum pulsed hard and deep into her.

Elaine was shocked that he had hit her so hard, but was cumming at the same time as him and felt him throb even harder at his action. Knowing that he was turned on by his control over her, she lay back and felt his hotness fill her up as she throbbed uncontrollably. He had stopped his pounding and was now holding her softly by the waist as his throbbing was slowing and his large cock was shrinking inside of her stretched hole. He bent down over her and began to kiss her gently on the lips as he slid the soft restraints off of her arms.

Exhausted but delighted to be free of the restraints on her wrists, she wrapped her arms around Chad. She had never felt anything like that before in her life and she longed for more of it. More of his control, of his safety, of knowing that he would be there to make her feel good and take care of her. She loved how in control he was of her and her body and how he didn't hesitate to take charge in order to get done what needed to be done. He had been fully prepared to tie her down and lord knows what else.

She wanted to be with him so much more and was dreading the end of the day.

Chad kissed her softly on the neck as he moved his way down to her ankles to free her of her final restraints.

"I hope that wasn't too much for you?" Chad said.

"I can be a pretty intense guy when it comes to certain things," he said matter-of-factly.

He moved back up and stroked the side of her face gently as she leaned in to kiss her more. Kissing him back and wrapping her tired legs around his waist, she pulled his ear close to her lips to whisper into it.

"I think I want to know what else you are intense about. I've never been.... Had that way. And I want you to have more of it," Elaine said to Chad as she began to kiss him on his neck.

"Oh, you're going to be able to have whatever you want if you keep being a good girl for me. I'm not exactly the easiest man to please though. Just to warn you. I do have expectations and requirements for those who are close to me. Especially for my women. Do you think that you are ready for something like that? Are you really ready for someone to be in control?" he said looking at her sincerely and what seemed like straight into her soul.

She looked out the window at the sun that was begin-ning to lower in the sky, oh how she dreaded the thought of going back to the boat or back to her real life. Why couldn't she just stay here forever instead? With this sexy, powerful man in paradise, fucking and playing for the rest of her days. It seemed like too much to wish for and she knew she was being selfish to even hope for it. Much less than a man like that would want to keep her around for any amount of time. She was probably just another plaything to a rich guy like him. In fact, the more that she thought about it, he probably swooned many girls the way that he had her. With his money and his fancy boat and his private tubing adventure. She knew deep down inside that his home had to be just as outrageous as the rest of his stuff and felt as though she could never compete or even last longer than a day or so in a world such as this. She was just one more go.

"We should get dressed and start to head toward the dockyard and check on your ship. Also, we should make sure that Kristy and Kyle are okay. But seeing as I didn't see the on our way up here I imagine they are doing just fine," Chad commented as he rolled off of her and off of the bed. He grabbed his trunks off of the floor and after wiping his cock dry with a towel slid them on. Elaine lay in the bed for a few moments.

"I don't want to move I feel so good. But I know you're right." She said as she began to pull herself to the edge of the bed.

Chad handed her a fresh towel.

"There's a clean robe in the closet that should work for you. Take your time and meet me on the deck once you've cleaned up," Chad said as he bent down to kiss her gently on the lips.

"I would let you lay there forever, but we need to check on your friend and the ship," and Chad walked out of the room leaving her alone inside of it.

Taking her time she slowly got up and walked over to

the mirrored closet door and opened it. Inside was an array of clothing nicely hung on padded hangers. In the middle hung four different robes of various lengths. She pulled out a plush black one and held it to her naked body. Rubbing the soft fabric against her skin. It was a bit big for her but she threw it on anyway and rolled up the sleeves over her arms.

Walking into his bathroom, she fixed up her hair before making her way down to the deck below.

She was walking out of the room when she noticed that the little chest was now slightly askew under the bed. Looking at the door to make sure that it was closed, she walked over to the bent and bent down. Running her hand over the ornately carved chest, she moved her fingers down to the finely crafted rod iron latches and lifted them, surprised that they came open freely this time. The top popped open and her mouth dropped open.

Inside of the chest was an array of sexual toys and devices along with various tubes of lotion and lube. On the very top lay the soft restraints he had just used on her. Shivers of excitement ran through her body. She honestly didn't even know what most of the things in the box were. Rummaging through the contents to the bottom she pulled out 3 older, blurry Polaroids. They were in a large, elaborate dungeon-like room. Or at least it seemed that way from the dark rock walls and the various rod iron contraptions and chains that seemed to decorate the walls. The subject of the first photo was a beautiful woman, tied up in her bra and underwear and bound to a chair in the middle of the room.

There was another woman who was straddled over her lap, completely naked, minus some clamps and chains attached to both of her nipples. She was poised to smother the woman in the chair with her large breasts, her nipples hard.

Elaine felt herself grow excited all over again at the thought of being tied down and helpless. So this was what he kept in his box.

"So looks like you're a nosey little bird," Chad said, somewhat sternly from the doorway.

Shocked, surprised, and feeling guilty, she dropped the pictures and closed her chest as her heart began to pound out of her chest.

CHAPTER 3

CHAD LOOKED at Elaine for a moment with a look of hurt and disappointment. Elaine felt terrified that she had been caught snooping and didn't even know what to expect from him.

"I really wish you wouldn't have done that," Chad said, somewhat sadly. "I suppose you would like me to take you back to the ship now?"

"Oh Chad, I'm so sorry, and no I don't want to go back yet unless you want me to go back," Elaine said, realizing that he thought that she would be mad or scared of him now.

"I'm not scared of this or you and I'm more than happy to stay. I'd even like to find out what the things in this box do exactly," Elaine said as she smiled at him seductively, running her hand over the smooth curves of the chest lid.

"You're not?" Chad asked incredulously. "No," Elaine said with firmness. "I'm not."

She walked over to him and wrapped her arms around his waist and reached up to kiss him on the lips. He bent down and returned her kiss, pulling her body close to his.

"I want you to show me," Elaine half demanded, half-asked as Chad began to nibble on her earlobe, sending chills down her arm.

"No," Chad said firmly, pulling away from her. She looked up at him, hurt and sad.

"Not now, we don't have time now and I want you to sleep on this and think if it's really something that you want to do with me. It's not like I'm going to tickle you with a feather once you are tied up. I will cause you pain, but I will never push things farther than you can handle. And I will always take the time to reward you for being good. Just as you will be punished for being bad or difficult. This isn't something that one just does with anyone. It requires trust and communication between all parties involved," Chad told her firmly looking deeply into her eyes.

"Well, but I..." Elaine began to protest.

"No buts, "Chad told her. "Have you ever been in a relationship like this before?" "No," Elaine responded dimly.

"Then you need to really think about what you are getting into before you decide that you want to do it. And then we can look into it if you decide it is a road you wish to travel down with me. It's no light commitment and I'm not willing to train another newbie only to find out that it's not really for you," Chad said curiously.

What exactly did that mean? She thought to herself. She had no words to say and just stared at the floor dismally.

He pulled her close and kissed her on the forehead.

"Don't worry beautiful. If it is something that you are really, truly thirsty for then I will not deny you. This is for your own protection, trust me. Let's go downstairs and see what's going on with the others and with your ship," Chad turned and holding her hand led the way out of his room and back down to the deck below.

She was crushed, but she followed him out to the main deck nonetheless. She could barely focus on the conversation as her mind kept wandering to the chest and the treasures contained within. Especially the photos. Oh, how she wished she had the time to look at all of them before Chad interrupted her. She was so curious to know what more he had in store. She really wasn't scared of any of it, but terribly excited. The more that she thought about the things that he might do to her the more that she grew excited. How could he question her and make her wait for something so amazing and intense? Before she knew it the yacht was in the main bay puttering past their stagnant cruise ship, still quiet in the waters.

"Hmmmm. Doesn't seem to be up and running again quite yet," Chad said.

"You ladies better go check and see what's going on with that boat regardless though."

Elaine looked outwardly downtrodden and Chad couldn't help but feel as though maybe he'd been a little rough on her.

"Tell you what. If you are still stuck in port tonight, why don't you give me a jingle? Jose should have already returned your items from tubing to the boat. If they aren't waiting for you in your room when you get back let me know immediately." Chad instructed as he began to walk them down off of the yacht. They reached the bottom of the stairs and Chad pulled her closer and gave her a big kiss.

"I don't want to chase you away. If you want to come to see me tonight, then I want you to. I have a little party organized at my place but my driver can pick you up and bring you at your leisure. If you want to come back, of course," Chad said to her.

She looked up at Chad with big wide eyes and pressed her body into his. "I hope the stupid boat stays broken down forever," Elaine whispered.

"Alright, go on now punk and I'll be waiting to hear from you," Chad said as he shooed her down the dock.

Elaine giggled and ran down the dock to catch up with her friend. Once they made their way back onto the boat Elaine and Kristy went to the customer service desk to find out what the deal was with the ship. They learned from Evrim that the ship was to be in port for one more day. Apparently, they were waiting for some part to be shipped overnight from back in the states, and then they could be back on their way. They were planning on adjusting the itinerary accordingly of course and had made up a few vouchers to please the unhappy passengers.

Elaine was overjoyed when she heard the news, but tried not to smile too big. "Let's go back to the room and freshen up for dinner," Kristy said.

"Okay, but I might want to go to have dinner with Chad. I want to see how I feel after a good shower and a small nap. It might just be the liquor talking still too." Elaine laughed.

"You are really smitten with him aren't you?" Kristy asked, teasingly. "You have no idea," Elaine replied.

"When I'm with him I completely forget that this was supposed to have been my honeymoon trip," Elaine said.

"I'm sure the wads of cash and the yacht don't hurt anything either," Kristy said. "That's not why I ---"Elaine started.

"Oh, I KNOW!! I'm just teasing you silly. Don't be so

sensitive," Kristy said as she slid her key into the door lock of the room.

"Do you want to shower first?" Elaine asked as they stepped into their cabin. Their belongings from the tubing trip had been neatly placed on their bed just as Chad had told them.

"Oh no, you can go first. Jeez, he really is good," Kristy said as she picked up her things from their tubing trip and began to put them away with the rest of her belongings.

Elaine stepped into the bathroom and turned on the water to the small shower, running until the heat began to put out steam before she stepped into a small tiled area. She lay back against the cool tile and let the warmer water wash over her naked body. Cleansing her of the day's sweat and sex. She couldn't stop thinking about how he had tied her down and what thrill she had gotten from his soft restraints and his violent pounding. How he had thrust himself inside of her so hard that she felt as though he might almost thrust himself into her stomach. She loved how he had taken control of her body and pushed her to limits she had never known before. She longed to know what else he had in store for her.

She was curious as to what else made him tick and turned on. She began to think about the contents of the chest and their many possible uses. She thought of the different bondages and restraints and of the photo with the woman tied up and the other woman with the chain and clamps hanging off of her large breasts. She longed to know more and have more done to her. She wasn't scared at all of Chad or of how he might be able to hurt her. She knew that he would never hurt her beyond what she could take.

Stepping out of the shower she felt more worked up and hotter than when she had stepped into it. She knew that she had to see Chad again and that night, before the ship left port tomorrow. She wanted to spend as much time with him as possible. Stepping out of the shower, she grabbed a towel and dried herself off. Wrapping it around her body, she walked out of the bathroom to tell her friend Kristy that she had decided to go have dinner with Chad.

Looking around the room, she didn't see her friend anywhere in sight. Walking out on the little balcony to confirm that she had gone, she turned her attention to getting dressed for the evening and then began to freak out because she had forgotten to get Chad's number from him. She wasn't even sure if her cell phone would work here. She hadn't planned on turning it on the whole time. Walking past the bed, she noticed a tiny envelope sitting on top of her belongings which had been returned from her tubing trip. Reaching down she picked it up and slip her finger underneath the lightly sealed flap and slid out the little card that was inside.

It read: *Elaine. Thank you so much for the wonderful time. Please accept this invitation to a little party I am hosting tonight. Dress in black-tie attire and the limo will Bentley will be waiting for you at the ship at 8:30 PM sharp. With all my heart... - C*

Her heart skipped a beat as she felt relief flood over her. Of course, he wouldn't just let her go without making sure that she could get ahold of him. Much less leave her hanging without ever seeing him again. That had been her biggest fear for a moment. She walked over to her closet and opened the door to try and figure out what to wear to the party.

She was shocked to find a brand new floor-length cock-tail dress hanging, brand new in the bag and perfectly her size. She pulled the gorgeous red dress out of the closet and held it up to her body.

Stepping into it, she zipped up the side zipper. It fit like a glove, enhancing her curves in all the right places and plunging low below the cleavage of her breasts. She was amazed that they managed to remain contained within the plunging neckline. Going back into the closet to pick a pair of black pumps out she noticed a brand new shoebox on the bottom of the closet floor and pulled it out.

There was another neat little envelope on the top of the shoe box.

It read: *I hope you don't mind that I took some liberties.... I thought that you would look very striking in these. No offense intended and I hope to see you soon. –C*

Offense? Not offended... enamored was more like it. She opened up the box and inside were a pair of beautiful black and red pumps, encrusted with little black jewels on their stiletto heels. And a tiny clutch which matched the shoes and dress perfectly. She completed her ensemble and looked in the mirror.

She felt like a million bucks or maybe even a billion. Checking the time on the small digital clock it read 8:31. Panicking, she grabbed her room key and scribbled a note quickly for Kristy so that she wouldn't worry about her being gone and rushed out of her room and down the ramp to the dock hoping that she hadn't missed her ride to the party. Reaching the bottom of the stairs, her heart sank when she realized there was no car waiting for her. She glanced at the time on her phone. It read 8:37. Perhaps she had been too late... Oh, if only she had been paying better attention to the time. The driver probably thought that she wasn't coming and left.

Heartbroken, she turned around and began to walk

back up the gangplank. She heard a car pull up behind her but was too busy fighting back tears to pay attention. The car honked and she turned her head to look at it, realizing it was the Bentley she immediately perked up and turned around. Running daintily over to the car in her heels, holding up the bottom of her dress so that she wouldn't get it dirty as she ran to the car. She had never felt such relief in her life.

The driver's window rolled down and the chauffeur stuck his head out. "Elaine?" he asked, unsure if she was his charge for the evening.

"Oh, yes... that's me! I thought I had missed you!" She said as she made her way up to the car.

The chauffeur stepped out of the car and held open the door for her as she climbed into the back seat. "I do apologize for being late. Someone's cows were on the road again between the estate and here.

Those things are always out at the most inconvenient of times. I'm so glad that you didn't give up on me. Chad would have been very sore with me," The chauffeur said as he closed her into the car.

He got back into the driver's seat and they drove off into the dark island night. After about 15 minutes of driving through the windy island streets, the car arrived at a large rod iron gate. Elaine was expecting him to roll down the window and punch in a code or put up a fob to make the gate open, but instead, it opened automatically/ the car cruised through the large gates and continued to wind down the light-up driveway through the island forest. Lined with little lights as they wound around the property for about 5 minutes before the trees gave way to a huge mansion lit up by spotlights and old-fashioned street lamps.

Elaine tried to contain the shock on her face. It looked

as though it had been built for a King, literally. The giant open courtyard that they were driving through on their way up to the magnificent house was accented with large marble statues and a beautiful lit-up fountain in the very middle of the driveway.

"The party began a little while ago, but Chad should be expecting you about now," said the chauffeur as he stepped out of the car once more. He walked back to Elaine's door, opened it for her, and held out his hand to help her out of the car. Taking her arm on his elbow, he walked her up the stairs to the giant double doors. They were hand-carved and reminded her tremendously of the chest, which she had gotten into. The chauffeur leaned forward to open the door and before he could reach the handle it swung open before them with, Chadstandingg behind them.

"You're late," he said in a booming voice.

Elaine looked up at him and smiled, "But it's not my fault," she began to protest.

"That's okay. Looking like that I would have been happy even if you showed up at the very end of the party," Chad said walking over to her and taking her hand.

"You look just like a dream my queen," Chad said as he bent down and kissed her gently on the top of her hand.

Elaine felt herself begin to blush but tried to distract herself with other goings-on.

"Thank you so much. You look amazing yourself. So where's the party at?" Elaine asked as she craned her neck to look down the long hallway in the direction of the music and revelry.

"This way... Come one!" Chad said, grabbing her hand and practically pulling her down the long hallway with its tall, arched ceilings. It was lined with expensive, oil paint-ings and antique furniture. The carpet upon which they walked was a beautifully ornate pattern resembling vines and flowers and felt 4 inches thick as she walked down it in her stilettos.

They reached the open doors of the ballroom and Elaine peeked her head around the doorway to see the room filled with guests in lavish ball gowns and expensive suits.

"And now, ladies and gentlemen, if you could please take a moment for me to introduce our host for the evening. You all love him, you all want to be him, and here he is, Mr. Chad Steffanopolis!!!" A large voice boomed over the microphone.

Elaine had no clue what was going and before she knew it Chad had taken her by the arm and the two of them were walking into the giant people-packed ballroom with all eyes on the both of them.

"And his gorgeous date for the evening, Ms. Elaine White," The voice continued.

The crowd applauded for them as Chad and she made their way through the crowd and up onto the DJ booth. The D.J. handed Chad the microphone.

"Thank you so much for coming tonight. It's not every day that I get to celebrate my birthday with such wonderful friends and colleagues. Thank you so very much. I love each and every one of you. Now....

Party on!!!" Chad said as he lifted his glass into the air and then took a swig of it. The crowd cheered as he handed the microphone back to the D.J. and climbed back out of the booth.

"Thanks, sorry to surprise you with that, but there's never really a good way to prepare a girl for that sort of thing. Best to just get the crash course. You did great though!" Chad said to her.

Elaine was looking at Chad somewhat angrily.

"Or not....." Chad said, unsure of why she was angry.

"You could have at least told me it was your birthday!!!" Elaine said aghast.

"Oh sweetie, I didn't want you to feel intimidated or like you had to get me anything. Besides having you for my birthday has been the best present anyone has ever given me," Chad said to her with his winning smile.

She could never stay mad at him, she thought to herself. Chad pulled her next to his side.

"Let's go get you a drink beautiful," he said as they began to work their way across the ballroom towards the bar in the corner.

Elaine couldn't help but notice the groups and clichés of couples and girls as they pointed to the two of them walking by, obviously whispering about them. She didn't let her phase her one bit though. She knew that they were jealous. How could they not be? They made their way to the bar and Chad ordered a glass of wine for Elaine and handed it to her.

"Shall we go dance?" Chad asked her as he dragged her off to the dance floor.

"Whatever the birthday boy desires," Elaine said with a smile as she followed him through the crowd.

Reaching the dance floor Chad pulled her close to his body and began to move to the rhythm of the music. He was a surprisingly good dancer Elaine thought. But then again he seemed to be excellent at most everything that he didn't so she wasn't sure why this would be any different. She took a big sip of her wine and lost herself in the rhythm of Chad's body moving against her own. She closed her eyes and leaned her head against his chest as they swayed back and forth. Relishing the moment as his strong hands worked up and down her back, brushing lightly over her ass. She blushed as he rested it there for a moment, pulling her crotch close against his, knowing that everyone was watching them as they moved together on the dance floor. She forgot about that as she returned the squeeze with her own free hand.

He leaned his head down to hers and whispered in her ear," I can't wait for all of these people to leave so I can have my favorite birthday present all to myself," he said as he ran a hand discreetly in between their two bodies. Grabbing her pussy through her expensive dress with force and pulling her against the hard bulge in his pants. She felt herself grow damp in between her soft thighs as he let go and moved his hands back to her waist.

They continued to dance until her glass of wine was empty and although she felt slightly buzzed she didn't argue a bit when he suggested they go get another drink from the bar. Once they were both situated with new drinks he began to walk away from the crowd toward one of the giant French doors in the ballroom.

"I thought we should get a breath of fresh air for a minute. Come this way," said Chad as he turned the golden handle of the large, windowed door and pushed it open. The salty, cool night air came rushing over them as they stepped outside onto the stone balcony. Almost as large as the ballroom itself and just as poshly decorated with large candelabras lighting the entire area. There were large pots with exotic tropical flowers blooming out of them and plush white oversized ottomans spread about for guests to lounge on. There were only a few other guests out on the patio, one couple leaning against the balcony wall sharing a cigarette. Another man and woman shared a white ottoman together talking and laughing quietly with each other while they swiveled their drinks in the air.

He led her to the edge of the balcony on the far corner of the other couple and behind one of the large planters. He roughly pinned her up against the wall, spilling a bit of both of their drinks with his unexpected motion. He planted his lips onto hers and forced them apart with his wet tongue, the alcohol on his breath filling Elaine's nose. She didn't fight him, but parted her lips and welcomed his tongue in with her own. Feeling his warm, soft wetness as they explored the inside of each other's mouths.

"I want you right now," Chad said gruffly in her ear as he began to hike up the long skirt of her fine gown. He shoved his hand inside of her panties and began to feel along her wet slit.

"Mmmmmm, already ready for me. I'm going to have you now and later I think. Is that the equivalent of having my cake and eating it too?" he said with a laugh as he began to kiss her roughly again. His thick fingers worked inside of her tight hole making it wetter and wetter as she squirmed against the wall. The roughness of the rocks, pulling at her done-up hair and scratching at the back of her neck as he pinned her against the wall. She felt her temperature rise as the blood rushed faster through her body, warming her face, her nipples, and pussy.

Chad grabbed her nipples hard through her gown as Elaine bit her lip to prevent a scream from escaping her lips.

"That's a good girl. We don't want anybody to hear you now. That would be terribly embarrassing," Chad told her softly as his hands worked her thong down and off of her as she stood against the wall. She felt him fumble with his belt and unzip his zipper, pulling his hard cock out and smashing it violently against her tight, wet lips. Frustrated that his cock wouldn't just slip into her he used one of his hands to loosen her tight wetness. Then he stuffed his solid, hard cock deep into her while he pressed one of his hands hard over her mouth to muffle the tiny scream he knew she wouldn't be able to suppress.

Elaine tried to scream, but couldn't as she felt his thickness fill up her pussy, his hand pressed so hard against her mouth that she couldn't even part her lips much less get out a sound. He had her pinned against the wall in a way that she couldn't move at all and solidly pound his cock into her pussy over and over again, Elaine's legs shaking and trembling as she came onto his cock so quickly she was embarrassed. He didn't stop but kept stuffing himself into her until he felt her cum on his shaft again, and then he allowed himself to release his load deep inside of her. Taking his hand off of her mouth and pulling himself out of her quickly he put his member back into his pants and zipped them back up as he leaned forward to kiss her softly on her lips. He bit her lower lip sharply, causing her to wince as he pulled away.

"Such a good girl. I've got a reward that you may have after the party," Chad said in her ear. He slid her panties back on underneath her long skirt and let it fall to the floor once more. Taking a step back, he looked her up and down twice and then stepped forward again and straightened her bangs, and wiped a bit of smeared lipstick from her lower lip.

"Much better. But we should still get you to the powder room so that you can freshen up," Chad insisted as he led her across the stone terrace and back through the beautiful doors into the noise and brightness of the ballroom festivities. He motioned to one of the servers.

"Could you please show my guest to the ladies' powder room," Chad requested of the quiet waitress? She nodded and began to walk off, leading the way to the restroom.

Elaine followed the server out of the ballroom and down the hallway, two doors to the women's powder room, and opened the door for her. She walked inside shocked to find it was exquisitely put together in the same manner as a French Baroque Powder room. Comprise mainly of white marble and golden mirrors. The first room consisted of two overstuffed white Chaise Lounges as well as two gold, claw-footed vanities. Each with their complete stock of any cosmetic product or feminine hygiene product that she could have possibly needed and a bunch that she would never need.

She felt a load of warm cum gush out of her, soaking her thin thong underneath her dress. She quickly grabbed a package of feminine wipes and opened the closet door, revealing a matching shower and changing room. Cursing it and closing the door behind her as the war, the cum began to travel down her inner thigh she hurried over to the other door to clean herself up before she could stain her beautiful gown.

Swinging it open she sighed with relief upon seeing the golden toiled and bench next to it. She hurried inside and closed the door behind her. Hiking up her skirt she was dismayed to see that some of her cum had dripped onto the inner lining, but was relieved to find that it hadn't gone all the way through. She pulled out a fresh wipe and began to clean herself up. Feeling more refreshed, she straightened her gown and went back out to the main powder room. Sitting down at one of the vanities she looked at herself in the golden frame of the mirror and truly felt like a queen. Her hair was still a bit mussed from their rough bout on the balcony so she took a moment to run a brush through it and make it look perfect again. Smiling, she realized she needed to refresh her lips as well and found the perfect shade of red to touch up her lips with. She smiled again at herself before she prepared to go back out to the party to find Chad amongst the large crowd. She felt like a queen for the night and wished that it would never end. Knowing that would probably never happen, she was bound to make the most of the night, smiled at herself again, and exited the powder room to traverse the hallway back to the ballroom.

She pulled open the large, heavy door and slipped into the loud room without anyone noticing. She looked around for a moment to try and locate Chad but couldn't find him anywhere. Not knowing what else to do she made her way over to the bar in the corner to order herself another drink.

'I'll have a glass of PinotGrigiorigio please," Elaine asked the bartender as her eyes searched the room for Chad. She began to panic at the thought of not finding him, but then reminded herself that she was at his home and chided herself quietly.

"And there she is now!" Chad's voice boomed from the other side of the bar. She had been so busy looking around the room for him that she hadn't even thought to look for him right here. She smiled at him as the bartender handed her another glass of wine and made her way around the bar to Chad's side.

"This is the gorgeous Elaine. I'm trying to convince her to stay... but she's not the easiest sell," Chad said as he showed her off to the small circle of three men whom he was standing with.

"You always did like a challenge Chad," Laughed the oldest man of the group.

"My name's Don. It's a pleasure to meet you," he said, sticking out his hand to shake hers firmly.

"Ah yes, and this is Zack and that is Mike. These are my

main business partners. Or shall I say partners in crime?"
Chad laughed as the rest of the men joined in.

"It's wonderful to meet you all," said Elaine.

"Well, gentlemen, I'd love to sit here and chat with you
all but I've got to say hello to some of my other guests before
the evening ends," Chad said as he excused them both from
the group.

"Only another hour or so my love until your reward.
Until then I have to say hello to a few more people, you
don't mind joining me do you? I'd like to introduce you,"
Chad requested of her.

"Anything for you, sir," Elaine cooed into his ear.

"That's my girl," Chad said proudly as he led her over to
another group of people and began the introductions and
the cheesy flattering of Elaine once more. They repeated
this cycle for what felt like forever. Elaine wasn't used to
such tedious social things and had never been at a party
which required her to mingle and interact with everyone
before. She was a bit out of her element, but just continued
to sip on her wine and laugh and smile as they went from
little group to little group. It felt like forever for the hour to
pass, but before she knew it the D.J. was announcing the
last song of the night and the options for the various guests
given their state of intoxication. Those who could drive
home still had their cars waiting for them outside. While
those who were more inebriated were taken to the guest
house on the property and made welcome there until the
next morning when they had sobered up.

They stood at the main doors to the mansion together as
they watched the last of Chad's guests leave his estate. He
pulled her close into him as they both waved goodbye to the
final car, honking as it drove out of sight. Chad pulled
Elaine inside and closed the large door behind her with a

slam. He pushed her roughly up against the carved wood, once again pushing his tongue deep down her throat. Pulling back abruptly he ran his fingers through her bangs, sweeping them out of her eyes.

"Are you ready for your reward my pet?" he asked her sweetly. "I've been ready," Elaine responded excitedly.

"Come with me," Chad said as he tugged on her hand gently and began to lead her down the hallway in the oppo-site direction of the ballroom. The hall grew darker as they got farther and farther away from the main entrance to his home. He walked over to the wall and flicked a switch on lighting up the hallway as it extended further into the dark-ness. Elaine felt as though the hallway would never end. Arriving at an opening in the stone hallway wall Chad flipped up another switch lighting up a stone stairway that descended downward.

Elaine's heart skipped a beat as her mind flashed to the Polaroid pictures she had found in the chest on the boat. Could this be his surprise for her? She had wanted to see the rest of those pictures so badly and now she was going to get to see the room itself she hoped. Holding her hand gently as he led the way down the stairs Chad smiled at her.

"I hope you're prepared for this," Chad said to her as they rounded the final turn of the spiral stone staircase. He flipped on one light switch on the wall beside the bottom of the stairs, lighting up the sparsely furnished and cavernous basement. The walls on the far side of the room seemed to be the same walls in the picture she had seen, with different black iron loops and hooks embedded deeply into the stone. There were even a couple of cells tucked away into the shadows of the huge room. Her nipples hardened, showing through the thing expensive fabric of her shirt, at the thought of the things that had gone on down here.

Chad noticed her hardened nipples and leaned forward to bite gently on them over her dress.

"I'm glad to see that you're excited for this. I haven't looked forward to something like this in a long time. Come this way," Chad told her as he led her to the far side of the room. Walking on the cold stone floor past the thick pillars which supported the massive house Elaine suddenly felt very small. She noticed sparse pieces of oddly shaped furniture placed here and there in shadowy corners or against a pillar.

As they neared the far end of the room, she noticed a large chest much like the little ones she had been finding, only this one was about 5 feet long and stood 3 and a half feet tall. It had the same ornate wooden carvings on it and iron latches. Her heart pounded as they walked over next to the chest, Chad kept dragging her past it and pushed her up against the concrete pillar next to the chest and began to kiss her deeply and hard again. Taking both of her hands in his own he raised them over her head until both wrists were next to each other and then held them both together tightly in one hand. Before she knew it, he had them both bound in the cold metal bracelet. She tried to pull them free but was stuck tight with them bound high above her head.

Chad stepped back and smiled at her as he ran his fingers down over her breasts and stomach, resting them briefly over her gap in between her thighs.

"You wanted to see what was in the chest. This is the chest that you want to see inside of then," Chad said, rubbing a hand over the lid before pulling it open and looking deep down inside of it. Elaine craned her neck to try and see the contents inside but was unable to.

"It's a shame you can't really see from there I guess I'll have to show them to you. But first, we need to get you ready," Chad said with a smile moving back over to her. He leaned forward to kiss her but bit her lip instead as his fingers pulled the zipper down the length of her back, allowing the gown to fall to the cold, gray floor in a pile of bright red fabric.

She felt the cold of the stone pillar against her naked back, only the small strips of fabric from her strapless bra and her thong to protect her from the scratchy chill. Chad removed her bra and thong next, leaving her completely vulnerable and helpless against the wall. Elaine felt herself begin to grow wet again, embarrassed that she had no way to hide it from Chad. He noticed her squirming and looked down between her legs to see the shine of her wet lips.

"So glad to see that you are as excited for this as I am," he said, walking slowly over to the chest, reaching inside her pulled something out, and enclosed it in the palm of his hand so that Elaine could not tell what it was. He walked back over to her and put his face close to hers.

"First, we need to work on your ability to be quiet," Chad said as he put his hand over her mouth and stuffed a soft round ball in between her unwilling lips. Quickly he strapped the ball onto her head and stepped back again to survey his work. He raised his hand and slapped her across the face unexpectedly and harder than Elaine had been prepared for. The smack of his hand stung her face and she tried to let out a muffled scream but was blocked by the object that was trapped into her mouth.

"Let's see what else I have for you in here," Chad said as he walked back over the chest. This time reaching in and pulling out a long chain. Walking back over to Elaine he grinned sadistically as he placed the ends of the chain over her nipples and began to clamp them down over her hard, pink buttons. She squirmed and wiggled as he twisted them tighter and tighter, stopping just before Elaine felt like she was going to scream again from the biting pleasure they caused.

"Hmmmm. You might be liking that a bit too much. Time for you to work for some of your pleasure," Chad said as he walked over to a crank on the other side of the pillar. He turned the large handle and Elaine heard heavy clinking from the links of the chain that was holding her up as her tired arms began to lower. Standing there with quite a bit of slack as Chad walked back over to the front of her.

"On your knees," he commanded.

She did as she was told without even thinking twice, her arms being held up above her again once again as she lowered herself to the floor, causing the chain to reach the capacity of its length. Chad grabbed her nicely done hair and unzipping his pants with the other hand, he stuffed his hard cock into Elaine's mouth as he began to fuck it harder than he had done on the yacht. Tears came to her eyes as she choked and sputtered on his hard thrusting, but she did what she could to keep up with his intense motions.

Just when she thought she could take no more he stopped and let go of her hair. Standing back, he smiled down at her, he reached down and grabbed on the chain which was attached to her throbbing nipples and pulled on it sharply, causing a stabbing pain; she stood quickly. Level with him now he pulled her closer to him very gingerly and leaned forward to kiss her softly on the lips. Her jaw was sore from how long he had been fucking her throat and her arms were weak from having held them above her head for so long but all she could think about was wanting more.

Chad reached up and unhooked her wrists from their metal constraints and led her over to a nearby cold stone bench. He lay down a fur over the top of the bench and then lay her down on her stomach as he pressed her body onto the bench with his own weight. He stretched out her arms to the bottom of the bench and then snapped them into two more metal bracelets that were attached to the floor. Forcing her to lay on the bench face down. He then got up and walked to the front of her and while she looked up at him with her large round eyes, unable to speak, he removed all of his clothing until he stood in front of her completely naked. Without saying a word he walked around out of her view and she felt goosebumps run through her body as he snapped a hard, metal bracelet onto each one of her ankles. Excitement flooded her body as she waited in anticipation for him to penetrate her. Instead, she felt his lips on her wet pussy lips and his tongue licking at the swollen clit, coercing more wetness out of her. He pulled back and then she felt him as he inserted the tip of his solid hard cock gently in between her lips.

Playing wither for a moment and teasing her soaked pussy he bounced the head of his cock in and out of her pussy until she writhed upon the bench in an attempt to push her pelvis further onto his cock.

"I suppose you've earned it by now," Chad said teasingly as he thrust himself deep into her wet hole.

Grabbing her by the hips, he began to work himself solidly in and out of her. Taking his hands, he forced down the small of her back and pulled her ass up towards his face, causing the head of his cock to slide over her G-spot with every push. She wiggled for what she could as she squirted her cum onto his cock once more. He slowed his thrusting as he throbbed inside of her, feeling the tight walls of her pussy as they gripped his shaft tightly amidst the throes of her cum.

He began to work himself up again, pounding into her

harder and harder as her legs trembled uncontrollably beneath him. He slapped her hard across the ass, leaving a bright red handprint, throbbing even harder as he built himself up to explode inside of her. He hit her on the ass again, harder this time leaving another handprint overlapping the other. Her ass was stinging and her pussy tightened upon his cock, in response, he let loose his large, hot load inside of her. Grabbing her hips, he held himself deep inside of her as he filled up her pussy with cum. She lay against the fur blanket on the hard bench and trembled with him as she came with him once more.

As soon as he quit throbbing he leaned forward and kissed Elaine gently on the back of the neck as he released the ball gag from her mouth. Reaching his arms down over hers, he unbound her wrist shackles and followed them by loosing her ankle shackles. Walking over to her with a large fur blanket he wrapped it around her as she sat up on the bench and held her close and he kissed her softly on the lips. Elaine had never known such intimacy and such passion in her life and wasn't sure how anyone couldn't like what she had experienced. Perhaps it was because they didn't know any better or maybe because they were just lame and boring. Whatever the reason was she felt like she was in heaven with this strong, sexy man and loved how he took care of her and controlled her. She never wanted to leave... Ever.

Chad looked at her deep in her eyes.

"I didn't hurt you, did I?" he asked her sincerely.

"No, not any more than I would want to be anyway," she said, looking back into his eyes with sincerity. "Mmm-mmm, that's my girl," Chad said, kissing her on the forehead.

"You know...... If you want to stay with me you can.

And if at any point you get tired of being here with me, I will send you back home at my expense of course. But I feel like we have an amazing connection and I'm willing to do what I have to.... to keep you here to explore "us" more. But I don't want you to stay if you find any of this in the slightest bit uncomfortable or weird. This is who I am and it's not going to change. I've lost more than one good woman because of it," Chad told her as he looked deep into her eyes once more.

Elaine didn't know what to say or think. She wanted to stay with him more than anything and his passion and veracity in the bedroom only excited her more. She wanted to figure out his puzzle, his enigma and she wanted to earn the right to know what was in those chests that he kept locked about all over his properties.

She thought about what to do and what Kristy would think. She knew what her friend would say. Hell, it was her fault that she had come on this cruise anyway.... And a good thing too.

"But what about my stuff on the ship?" Elaine asked.

"We can have the Jose go and fetch it in the morning before the ship leaves. I imagine that you'll want to get word to Kristy that you are going to be staying here as well. That way she doesn't think I killed you or something horrible like that," Chad suggested.

"Oh, yup. That might be a good idea too. You've got everything figured out. I think maybe even me," Elaine said jokingly.

"One could only hope to have such an enigma figured out so quickly. I imagine it's going to take us a little while to really get to know each other. Besides, I've got so much to show you and help you discover. We only touched the tippy top of the chest," Chad said with a smile as he motioned toward the large open box.

Elaine looked over at the huge box and smiled, she was eager to discover whatever he had to show her and had a strong desire to learn how to please him and make him happy in return. She thought about her job back at home and the things which she would have to deal with if she wound up staying, like her apartment and finances, and... she stopped her train of thought as she realized she was getting way too far ahead of herself. She could always get another job and if for some reason it looked like she was going to be here longer than when rent was due next she was sure that Chad would help her take care of everything. He had done such a great job of that so far.

"Okay, I'll stay," Elaine said as she gave in to her heart and Chad's wishes even against her better logic.

"Really?!" Chad exclaimed. "That's the best birthday present I've had in years. Let's head up to my bedroom. I'll have Jose take care of all the details first thing in the morning. I couldn't be more pleased with your decision my queen," said Chad, extending his hand out for her to hold onto as he led them out of the dungeon and up the stairs to his bedroom.

ABOUT THE AUTHOR

Helana Parkins is an emerging erotica author of many erotica kinks and sub-genres. Be sure to check out other books and leave a review if this story got you hot!

Visit my blog at Helana Parkins Blog

Join my newsletter for exclusive previews Helana Parkins Newsletter

Sign up for Free Stories from Xplicit Press Authors

Xplicit Press Author Updates

Like Xplicit Press on Facebook

Follow Xplicit Press on Twitter

Readers: I want to expand a few of the stories to see where the characters can be explored further. If there are any of the stories that you would like to read more about again, I'd love to hear from you!

Keep In Touch
Helana Parkins
info@helanaparkins.com